I Don't Want To Go To Bed!

Tony Ross

More Little Princess books

I Want My Potty

Wash Your Hands!

I Want My Pacifier

First American edition 2004
By Kane/Miller Book Publishers, Inc.
La Jolla, California

First published in 2003 by Andersen Press Ltd., Great Britain
Text and illustrations copyright © Tony Ross, 2003

Kane/Miller Book Publishers
P.O. Box 8515
La Jolla, CA 92038
www.kanemiller.com

Library of Congress Control Number: 2004100849

Printed and bound in China by Regent Publishing Services Ltd.

1 2 3 4 5 6 7 8 9 10

ISBN 1-929132-66-2

I Don't Want To Go To Bed!

Tony Ross

Kane/Miller
BOOK PUBLISHERS

"Why do I have to go to bed when I'm not tired and get up when I am?" asked the Little Princess.

"I don't **WANT** to go to bed!" she said.

"Bed is good for you," said the Doctor,
taking her upstairs. "Sleep is even better."

But the Little Princess came straight down again.
"I DON'T WANT TO GO TO BED!" she said.

"I WANT A GLASS OF WATER!"

"There you are," said the Queen.
"Sleepy, sleepy tighty."

"DAAAAAD!"

"You don't want another glass of water?" asked the King.
"No," said the Little Princess. "Gilbert does."

"Nighty, nighty," said the King. "Sleepy tighty, Gilbert."
"Don't go!" said the Little Princess. "There's a monster in the closet."

"There's no such thing as monsters, and there are none in the closet," said the King, closing the bedroom door.

"Dad!" shouted the Little Princess. "What is it now?" asked the King. "You're not still frightened of monsters?"

"Of course I'm not," said the Little Princess.
"Gilbert is. He says there's one under the bed."

"No there isn't," said the King, creeping out of the bedroom. "There are no such things."

"Stop her!" shouted the Queen. "She's escaped." **"I DON'T WANT TO GO TO BED!"** said the Little Princess. "Why not?" asked the Queen.

"There's a spider over my bed...
...and it's got hairy legs."

"Daddy's got hairy legs, and he's nice," said the Queen.

At last the Little Princess went to bed.

Later, when the King went in to kiss her
goodnight, her bed was empty.

Everybody hunted high…

…and low, until…

"Here she is," said the Maid.
"She's keeping Gilbert and the cat safe from spiders and monsters."

The next morning, the Little Princess got up and yawned a yawn.
"I'm tired," she said…

"I want to go to bed."